# My Winter Vacation
# A Memory - Box™
# Activity Book

Created by Jane May

Illustrated by Marty Norman

and Starring

_____

(your name)

Abbeville Press · Publishers · New York

*To monkey*

      \*     \*     \*

*Thanks to Suzanne and Alison for their invaluable assistance, and to the folks at the Stowe Area Association, as well as Topnotch at Stowe Resort, for their encouraging words.*

Art Director: Renée Khatami
Designer: Laura Ferguson
Editor: Alison Mitchell
Consulting Editor: Suzanne Weyn
Copy Chief: Robin James
Production Manager: Dana Cole

First edition

ʿBN 0-89659-874-8   Book not available separately.

# This Memory-Box™ Activity Book belongs to

_____,
(your name)

**who is _____ years old and lives at**

_____

_____

# Contents

# How to Use Your Memory-Box™ Activity Book

Dear Kids,

"What's all this about a Memory Box?" you may ask. "And what does it have to do with my winter vacation?"

Well, here's the scoop. As you slide and whizz and whoop through your winter wonderland, don't let the memories melt away. With this Memory-Box™ Activity Book you can make a special kind of journal and scrapbook of your trip. When the book is finished, this record of your adventures will be a little like a time capsule, but don't stick it in a snowbank! Show it off to all your family and friends!

In order to create this masterpiece, you'll need to act like a reporter and write down your observations of the people, places, and interesting things you encounter during your vacation. Get into the habit of collecting stuff you come across in your journey—transportation ticket receipts, trail maps, ski passes, postcards, brochures, matchbook covers, maps, decals, printed napkins, and such—because any and all souvenirs you'd like to save and remember can be glued or taped into the book or kept in the box. Add your own illustrations by drawing or photographing the snowy mountain sights.

I'll be with you all along the way with lots of suggestions. I've also thrown in some fun facts to astound and impress your traveling companions. If you're stumped on how to complete a particular section—no problem. Just take your time, come back to it later, or skip it entirely. If some of these pages don't apply to *your* winter vacation—after all, it's impossible to do *everything* in a single trip—just move along to the next section. The most important thing about your Memory-Box™ book is to enjoy it. Have a blast!

You'll need these tools of the trade (if you like, you can store these things in the box and carry the book separately):

- *Pencils.* Sometimes it's wise to pencil in your ideas before preserving them in ink. This gives you the flexibility to change your mind.
- *Crayons or felt-tip pens.* Make this book as bright and colorful as your winter wear!
- *Scissors.* Use them to cut brochures or photos to fit in your book.
- *Glue or transparent tape.* These work better than chewing gum for sticking things to the page.
- *An obliging adult or two.* These are helpful and fun to have around while frolicking on the high peaks. You might like to invite them to participate in Memory-Box™ projects—I'll bet they'd get a kick out of it, too.

One last suggestion before you head for the hills. Do skim through the table of contents and the rest of the book so you know what's up ahead. That way, you can skip around as the spirit (or your itinerary) moves you. Ready? Bundle up and go for it! Have a great vacation!

Sentimentally yours,

Jane May

Jane May

# You're on Your Way!

You're on your way! Whether you're traveling by car, bus, train, plane, or snowmobile, record your memories here! As you journey toward the snow-covered mountains, the story of your winter vacation begins.

We left home at about _____ o'clock on _____,

_____, 19\_\_\_\_, headed for a winter wonderland called

_____.

My traveling companions are _____

_____.

We traveled by (circle the ones that are true for you)

    airplane    train    car    helicopter    bus    snowmobile

    one-horse open sleigh    dogsled    cable car    snowcat

    other: _____

During our journey the weather was mostly _____,

and our mood was _____.

> For long trips, pack a bag with some of the following things: healthy munchies, something to drink, books and magazines, portable games, cassette tapes (try stories as well as music), a family songbook, and a blank pad and pencil for drawing, Tic-tac-toe, and other pencil games.

# Getting There-By Car!

For the most part, the traffic was _____,

and our average cruising speed was _____ miles per hour. Along the

way, we saw _____

_____

_____.

We stopped for a rest at _____.

We traveled through these states: _____

_____,

crossed these bridges: _____

_____,

and went through these tunnels: _____

_____.

To pass the time, I _____

_____

_____.

Did you ever play the Alphabet Game? Divide the
passengers (not counting the driver, who's busy) into two
teams, one for each side of the road. Each team looks out
the windows on their side, searching for the letter "A"
on a sign, billboard, mailbox, bumper sticker, or license
plate. As soon as a player finds one, he or she calls it out
and that player's team moves on to search for "B." (The
other team still has to find an "A" on *its* side.) The first
team to call out all the letters of the alphabet—one at a
time and in order—wins. (By the way, Q and Z can be
rough going, and license plates of cars in the same lane
as your car don't count for either side.)

The most exciting or hair-raising part of the trip was when _____

_____

_____.

The best thing about traveling by car is _____

_____

_____.

In all, we traveled _____ miles in _____ hours.


# Getting There – By Train!

We pulled out of _____ Station at precisely _____ o'clock.

Our train was number _____ of the _____ Railroad.
<br>(name of railroad company)

This train is also known as _____.
<br>(The California Zephyr? The Montrealer?)

It had _____ cars and made _____ stops between

_____ and _____
<br>(your departure point)      (your destination)

As we rolled along, we _____

_____

_____.

From the window, I saw _____

_____

_____.

We pulled into _____ Station at precisely _____ o'clock.

The best thing about traveling by train is _____

_____.

Use this space for your ticket stub, napkins from the snack bar, or other souvenirs.

# Getting There-By Plane!

For information about your airplane and the flight, check the seat pocket in front of you, listen to the announcements that the pilot or attendants make, and if you still have questions, don't be shy to ask!

Our flight was number _____ on _____, and it
(name of airline)

left _____ Airport at _____ o'clock. It

was/wasn't on time. My seat number was _____.
(circle)

I enjoyed/didn't enjoy the take-off because _____
(circle)

_____.

Our plane was a _____ with _____ engines, and our
(type and model number)

average speed was _____ miles per hour. Our average altitude

was _____ feet.

On the way, we flew over _____

_____

_____.

From the window, I saw _____

_____

_____.

During the flight, I (circle)

watched the in-flight movie, which was called _____

_____. I thought it was _____.

read a book/magazine, titled _____.
(circle)

did crossword puzzles.

slept.

played a game of _____ with _____.

The in-flight meal was _____

_____.

I liked/didn't like it, especially the _____.
(circle)

This is what else I did to pass the time while we were in the air: _____

_____

_____

The best part of the flight was _____

_____,

because _____.

We landed at _____ Airport at _____ o'clock.

We'll continue on to our vacation destination by (circle)

taxi     bus     car     van     train     sleigh     other: _____

13

# Getting There

These pages are for ticket stubs, toll receipts, airline brochures, autographs of train conductors or airline attendants, and anything else you collected en route.

# First Impressions

# This Must Be the Place!

Three. Two. One. Contact!

We arrived at last at _____ o'clock in the _____

on _____, _____, 19 \_\_\_.

We are in the _____ Mountain area in the state

of _____.

The closest town is _____, and the nearest major city

is _____, which is about _____ miles away.

We'll be staying in a (circle)

| | |
|---|---|
| hotel | A-frame cottage |
| motel | house |
| ski lodge | chalet |
| condominium | igloo |
| country inn | snowbank |
| converted barn | other: _____ |

The name of the place is _____, and

the address is _____

_____.

Our room number (if staying in a hotel or motel) is _____.

When I look outside, this is what I see: _____

_____

_____

# This Must Be the Place!

Some of the special features of our home away from home:

(A fireplace? A hot tub? A feather bed and goosedown quilt?)_____

_____

_____

_____

So far, I like/don't like this place because _____
(circle)

_____

_____

_____

_____

_____

To get to the slopes/cross-country trails, we (circle)

    just step outside our front door    travel to the next canyon

    drive a few miles down the road    hike through the woods

    other: _____

Being in the mountains makes me feel _____

_____

_____

_____

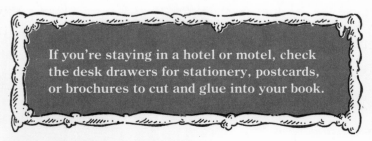

If you're staying in a hotel or motel, check the desk drawers for stationery, postcards, or brochures to cut and glue into your book.

This space is reserved for memories of your vacation accommodations—use souvenirs, photos, or drawings.

# The First Day

So! How was your first day of vacation?

We got up at _____ o'clock and had _____

_____ for breakfast.

Then we _____

_____

_____

_____.

Later on, we _____

_____

_____.

The weather was mostly _____.

By sundown, we were all _____, so we

_____

_____.

Judging from the first day, I think the rest of this vacation will be _____

_____.

I can't wait to _____

_____.

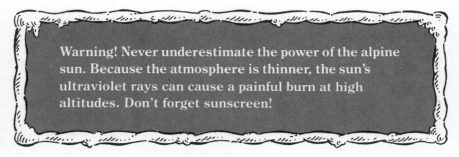

Warning! Never underestimate the power of the alpine sun. Because the atmosphere is thinner, the sun's ultraviolet rays can cause a painful burn at high altitudes. Don't forget sunscreen!

Here are some photographs or drawings of me and my traveling companions on our first day out.

# Snow Glory

# An Homage to Snow

Think of summer and you picture trees and flowers and sparkling beaches. Think of fall and you see brilliant shades of red, brown, and orange. But think of winter, especially winter in the mountains, and it's snow that comes to mind. Rather than take that white stuff for granted, let's pay a little homage to snow.

What *is* snow, anyway? Well, it's a truly chilling tale. Let's be scientific for just a minute.

The air in clouds contains lots of tiny droplets of water. When the air temperature is very cold, the droplets turn to ice. As the tiny pieces of ice begin to fall through the air, more water freezes on them and the crystals grow bigger. Eventually, the ice crystals clump together to form snowflakes, and when the flakes are heavy enough, they fall to the ground.

Now, snowflakes come in over 8,000 shapes of crystals. Scientists have classified those shapes into seven basic categories—plates, stellars, columns, needles, spatial dendrites, capped columns, and irregular crystals—but, like grains of sand, no two snowflakes are exactly alike.

Lots of things affect the size and shape of snowflakes—the amount of moisture in the air, the presence of dust particles in the forming crystals, and the temperature at which they are formed. After the snow has fallen to the ground, it continues to change as the crystals settle, melt, and refreeze. For example, "powder snow" (the stuff we all dream about) is made up of very large snowflakes that have fallen to the ground and continued to squiggle and squirm. All this action causes air to get trapped in between the snowy layers, and the result is powdery snow that's light, airy, and dry.

# Snowflakes

Mr. Wilson Alwyn Bentley was known as the "Snowflake Man" of Jericho, Vermont. For fifty years, he carefully studied and photographed these "falling jewels" through the lens of his compound microscope. His photographs were published in 1931 and have been displayed in museums. Try looking at snowflakes with the aid of a magnifying glass (or a microscope, if one is available), and try to identify the snowflake type. Who knows, maybe you'll get hooked on snowflakes, too.

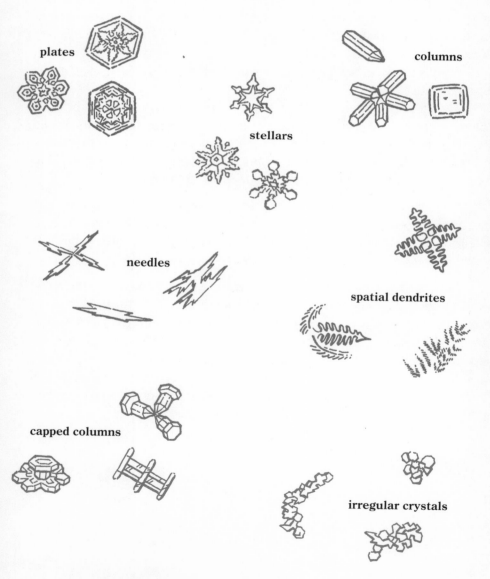

plates

columns

stellars

needles

spatial dendrites

capped columns

irregular crystals

Use this space for *your* tribute to snow. Write a poem or story, take a beautiful photograph of a snowy landscape, or draw a page full of intricately patterned snowflakes.

# More Frosty Facts

- Most snowflakes are hexagonal (six-sided) and symmetrical.

- Snow crystals are actually transparent—they only *appear* white because their complex surfaces reflect so much light.

- The heaviest snowfalls do not happen when the temperatures get really frosty. The thermometer has to be between 24 and 30 degrees Fahrenheit for a wing-dinger of a storm to occur.

- Are you never satisfied with the amount of snow on the ground? Then you should have been in Silver Lake, Colorado, in 1921. It snowed 75.8 inches in 24 hours!

- Or, if you prefer giant snowflakes, head for Topeka, Kansas. The snowflakes there measure up to 2½ inches in diameter.

- By the way, thirty inches of dry powdery snowflakes are equivalent to only one inch of rain!

# Paper Snowflakes

Here's how to make the *best* paper snowflakes ever!

1. Trace around a small glass (or use a compass) to draw a circle on white paper.

2. Fold the circle in half, then in thirds. Your paper will now look like a slice of pie.

3. Cut out little shapes—triangles, half-moons, thin slits—along the creases and open edge of the pie. Make them as simple or as complicated as you like: more cuts make a lacier snowflake, fewer cuts make the snowflake more abstract.

4. Carefully unfold the circle (the cut edges may tend to stick together). Presto!

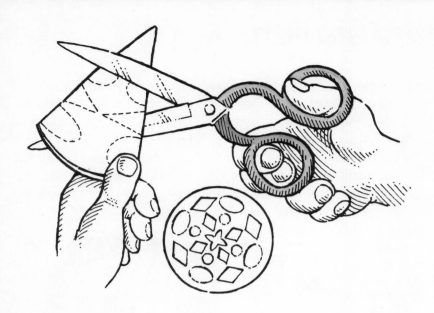

Glue in a snowflake below. Paper snowflakes make great greeting cards when you glue them to brightly colored construction paper.

# Dressing for the Occasion

To enjoy the great outdoors in winter, you have to dress for the weather. Don't let the morning sunshine fool you—it will be much colder and windier on lifts, slopes, or in the shade of wooded trails. (Downhill skiers should always check the summit temperature before setting off for the day.) Never sacrifice warmth for high fashion. And take a tip from the Eskimos! Wear loose-fitting layers that trap warm air and keep you insulated from the cold. If the day warms up—or if *you* warm up from cross-country skiing or other energetic activities—just peel off one layer and stay comfortable all day.

Did you know that 50% of lost body heat escapes from the top of your head?
You may *look* cool hatless, but you'll feel that way too!

Here's a list of winter wear to help you keep toasty. You can also immortalize *your* favorite winter outfit by writing down the types, colors, and sizes of its components.

Long (thermal) underwear: _____

Socks: _____

Turtleneck or flannel shirt: _____

Sweater(s): _____

Ski pants or bib or jeans: _____

Windbreaker or down vest: _____

Insulated parka: _____

Boots: _____

Mittens or gloves: _____

Scarf or face mask: _____

Hat: _____

Polarized sunglasses or goggles: _____

Other: _____

Time yourself. How long does it take you to get dressed?

_____ hours/minutes/seconds.
(circle)

Use this space for a photograph or drawing of you all dressed and ready for a day in the snow. Or use the extra pages at the back of the book to make a collage of magazine pictures showing clothing or sports equipment you'd like to own.

# Fun in the Snow

When there's snow on the ground, no kid—and very few grown-ups—can resist the urge to go out and pack it, throw it, mold it, play with it, and jump around in it. You can build snowpeople, forts, and igloos. You can make snow angels. And, yes, you can have a snowball fight. (But no iceballs allowed! And *never* aim for the face or head!)

Here are some tips for creating spiffy snow structures:

- To make huge snowballs (for snowmen or other sculptures), start small. Roll a snowball over and over in fresh snow till it grows bigger and bigger and bigger and bigger and. . . .

- For great building blocks, pack snow into egg cartons, shoe boxes, or other containers. Pour a little water over the snow and wait for it to freeze. Turn the containers upside down, and there you have it—snow bricks! Use extra snow as "mortar" to stick them together.

- Spritz your snow sculpture with a spray-bottle full of water to preserve the masterpiece for a longer time.

- Snow shovels are handy for making forts, and forks, spoons, and window scrapers are good tools for sculpting.

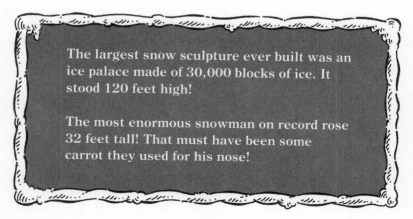

The largest snow sculpture ever built was an ice palace made of 30,000 blocks of ice. It stood 120 feet high!

The most enormous snowman on record rose 32 feet tall! That must have been some carrot they used for his nose!

Here's more room for your snowy memories. Snap a photo of a snow creation, or recount a snowball battle in words and/or pictures.

Moving!

Whether you're schussing down a mountainside or skating on a frozen lake, gliding through the forest on cross-country skis or roaring up a canyon in a snowmobile, you are moving!

Many winter sports—like sledding, skiing, skating, and snowshoeing—are as old as the hills themselves. Others—snowmobiling, skibobbing, and snowboarding—were invented just a few years ago. In the 21st century, who knows what new and zany ways you'll be able to zoom around on frozen turf!

Remember, safety is the first priority when it comes to winter sports. Always keep your speed under control, be aware of the other movers and shakers around you, and don't attempt *any* fancy flips or daredevil tricks until you—and your instructor—are *sure* you're ready for them. And when you start to feel tired, call it a day. Most accidents occur toward sundown, when muscles are overworked and the light is beginning to fade.

Keep track of your thrills, chills, spills, and athletic adventures in the pages that follow. Save lift tickets, trail maps, and other souvenirs, take plenty of photographs, and report your achievements in sparkling detail.

Be warm, be safe, and be a sport! Have a great time!

# Skiing

Skiing developed in Scandinavia thousands of years ago. In those days, skis looked rather like snowshoes and were used as a form of transportation in the winter months—skiing was simply faster and easier than trudging through deep snow. Soldiers even wore skis to battle, and hunters used them while stalking their prey.

Competitive skiing began in the mid-1800s in Norway, Austria, and California, where the first cross-country, downhill, and ski jumping events were held. Advancements in ski equipment—particularly bindings—and the refinement of ski techniques increased the sport's popularity at the turn of the century. Today, skiers can be found schussing down mountains in the most unlikely of locations—places like Hawaii, Israel, Africa, and India! In fact, it's estimated that more than 30 million people worldwide take to the slopes each year!

Whether you prefer Alpine (downhill) skiing or Nordic (cross-country) skiing, record your adventures herein!

# Ski Facts

 The earliest-known ski was unearthed in Hoting, Sweden. Scientists estimate that it is 4,500 years old!

 The 1932 Winter Olympics were held at Lake Placid, New York. These games provided the spark that ignited America's passion for skiing.

 The busiest ski complex in the country is in Mammoth, California. In a year, up to and perhaps over one and a half million skiers visit it.

 Stowe, Vermont, hosts the oldest annual cross-country race in the U.S. It's called the Stowe Derby and takes place in February.

# Ski School Days

Ever since Austrian Hannes Schneider, the father of modern skiing, invented the stem turn and the stem christie, ski schools have been an important force in improving and popularizing both downhill and cross-country skiing. The first American ski school opened at Sugar Hill in Franconia, New Hampshire, in 1929. Lessons back then were a buck apiece. Boy, have times changed!

If you're enrolled in a ski school or take a lesson during your vacation, fill in the particulars on the next two pages.

The name of my ski school is _____

_____.

The names of my instructors are _____

_____

_____.

The method of skiing taught here is _____

_____

_____.

There are _____ kids in my group and our class is called _____

_____

This is what a typical lesson is like:

We start at _____ o'clock and finish around _____ o'clock.

We head out to _____

and begin by _____

_____

_____.

Then we _____

_____

_____

_____.

We also practice _____

_____

_____

_____

_____.

Important tips I want to remember:

_____

_____

_____

_____

_____

All in all, I think ski school has been (circle)

    tons of fun        a huge success—I've really improved

    a waste of time      very useful, but a little dull      very challenging

    other: _____

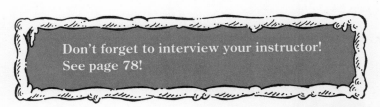

Don't forget to interview your instructor!
See page 78!

# Downhill Skiing

"The two most important things for a successful beginning on skis are confidence and bent knees."
Richard Lyttle,
*The Complete Beginner's Guide to Skiing*

I've been skiing for _____ years/months/days. I started at the
(circle)

age of _____, and I learned/I'm learning by _____
(circle)

_____

at _____.

I make these kinds of turns: _____, and stop myself

by _____.

I can also do some (circle)

mogul jumping     schussing     racing maneuvers     tip rolls

royal Christies     daffy and spread eagles     helicopter spins

downhill Charlestons     back scratchers     ski ballet moves

other: _____

When I fall down, I _____

_____.

I consider myself to be (circle)

a beginner     a novice     an intermediate skier     an advanced skier

an expert     an advanced expert

I ski best on (circle)

gentle slopes     wide slopes     intermediate trails

steep terrain     mogul fields     chutes     bowls

quiet wooded trails     glades     racing hills     other: _____

What I like best about skiing is _____

_____

_____

_____

_____.

What I *don't* like is _____

_____

_____.

As a skier, I think my strengths are _____

_____

_____.

My weak points are _____

_____.

39

During this vacation/ski season, I'd like to learn how to ＿＿＿＿＿＿＿＿＿
(circle)

＿＿＿＿＿＿＿＿＿＿＿＿＿＿＿＿＿＿＿＿＿＿＿＿＿＿＿＿＿＿＿＿

＿＿＿＿＿＿＿＿＿＿＿＿＿＿＿＿＿＿＿＿＿＿＿＿＿＿＿＿＿＿＿.

On the average, I ski this many days a year: ＿＿＿＿＿＿＿＿＿＿＿＿

# Equipment

How do you gear up? Record all the particulars.

*Boots*

    Size: ＿＿＿＿＿＿＿＿＿＿＿＿＿＿＿＿＿＿＿＿

    Brand: ＿＿＿＿＿＿＿＿＿＿＿＿＿＿＿＿＿＿

    Style: ＿＿＿＿＿＿＿＿＿＿＿＿＿＿＿＿＿＿＿

    Type of fastening: ＿＿＿＿＿＿＿＿＿＿＿

    Color: ＿＿＿＿＿＿＿＿＿＿＿＿＿＿＿＿＿＿

    Comfortable? ＿＿＿＿＿＿＿＿＿＿＿＿＿＿

*Bindings*

    Type: ＿＿＿＿＿＿＿＿＿＿＿＿＿＿＿＿＿＿

    Brand: ＿＿＿＿＿＿＿＿＿＿＿＿＿＿＿＿＿＿

    Safety device:  straps/brakes
                   (circle)

*Skis*

    Brand: ＿＿＿＿＿＿＿＿＿＿＿＿＿＿＿＿＿＿

    Style or model: ＿＿＿＿＿＿＿＿＿＿＿＿＿

    Length: ＿＿＿＿＿＿＿＿＿＿＿＿＿＿＿＿＿

*Poles*

    Brand: ＿＿＿＿＿＿＿＿＿＿＿＿＿＿＿＿＿＿

    Length: ＿＿＿＿＿＿＿＿＿＿＿＿＿＿＿＿＿

Use this page for a drawing or photograph of you on skis.

If you're aching to race, ask someone at the ski center about NASTAR. This organization sponsors competitions for recreational skiers. All entrants are age- and ability-matched.

Use this page for a panoramic view of the mountains—a postcard, a photograph, a picture from the ski center brochure, or a drawing.

# Ski Safety

- Be courteous to other skiers. Don't cut them off or bombard them.

- Don't ski like a speed-crazed baboon. Ski under control.

- Plough someone down by accident? Help them get up or help retrieve lost equipment.

- If you fall, get up as quickly as possible. There are other spots for rest.

- Be careful when skiing through snowmaking areas.

- Wait your turn patiently in lift lines and be polite to attendants (a "thanks" would be really nice).

- Don't play chicken with snow cats.

- Don't litter. Someone may fall on your discarded trash.

- Always be aware of people around you when carting your skis. You don't want to bop someone on the head.

- Always ski with a companion.

- Never ski in posted areas or on trails marked "danger."

- Don't try to stop a runaway ski, but warn others of it.

- And always check with each particular ski area for a list of their safety rules.

# Downhill Mountain Information

It's time to get better acquainted with your friendly local mountains. A lot of the information you'll need can be found in trail maps and brochures, which you can pick up at the base lodge, a hotel lobby, or a tourist office. Or ask a member of the ski center staff. Don't forget to save your lift ticket(s) so you can paste it into this book.

Name of the mountain or ski area:

_____

It's situated in the _____ Mountain chain.

The vertical drop of the ski area is _____ feet. The summit elevation is

_____ feet.

The total number of trails is _____, with _____ beginner slopes,

_____ intermediate, and _____ advanced trails.

The total number of "skiable acres" is _____.

These are the different ways to get up this mountain (circle):

    T-bar       J-bar       poma       rope tow       gondola

    chair lift (double, triple, quadruple)       cable car       ski train

    funiculaire       helicopter       other: _____

This many skiers can be transported up the mountain in an hour: _____

The longest run stretches for _____ miles.

This mountain is (circle)

    well-groomed       not well-groomed       not groomed at all

"It's not the size [of the mountain] it's the punch!"
Bill Hubbard, in *Ski Magazine*

In season, the average temperature at the base of the mountain is

_____ degrees Celsius/Fahrenheit.
        (circle)

The average temperature at the summit is _____ degrees.

The skiing season here lasts from the month of _____ until

_____.

The condition of the snow tends to be (circle)

    deep powder    packed powder    icy    corn snow

    crusty    "Sierra cement"    sugar snow

    granular    frozen granular    loose granular    wet snow

    windblown snow    other: _____

This mountain has some of the following trails (circle):

    winding wooded paths    snow bowls    bunny slopes

    glades (slopes with lots of trees to ski around and through)

    wide, open slopes    chutes    gullies    super-steep terrain

    mogul fields    narrow traverses

    other: _____

My favorite trails are named _____

_____.

I like them because _____

_____.

The trails that make me shudder and shake are _____

_____, because

_____.

The best thing about skiing on this mountain is _____

_____

_____

_____.

45

# Downhill Mountain Information

Use this space for pasting in your trail map. You can circle or trace the areas you skied. (If the map's too big to paste in, store it in your Memory Box.)

Snowmaking is essential for some ski centers. Here's how they make their *own* weather: Water and compressed air are mixed together in a sort of washing machine, then shot out by the hose pipe of a compressor. In order for this concoction to come out as snow, the air must be cold and dry enough. This kind of artificially produced snow actually lasts longer than the real thing!

Use this space for lift tickets and ski passes when you're finished using them.

In 19 _____, the price of a lift ticket at _____ Mountain is

$_____.

A "monadnock" is a free-standing mountain that has no
relation to any other mountains or mountain chain.
There aren't a lot of ski mountains like this, but two rare
examples are Burke Mountain in Vermont and Sugarloaf
in Maine.

# My Adventures, Explorations, and Progress on Downhill Skis

As with most things in life, practice makes perfect. Chart your skiing progress here.

First day out: _____

_____

_____

Second day: _____

_____

_____

Third day: _____

_____

_____

Fourth day: _____

_____

_____

Fifth day: _____

_____

_____

Sixth day: _____

_____

_____

**Remember, control is the key to your safety and everybody else's.**

In words and/or pictures, describe a particularly thrilling experience.

Use these pages for photographs of you skiing, additional trail maps, pictures from the ski center brochure, postcards, and other mementos of your downhill adventures.

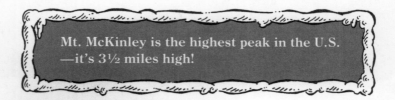

Mt. McKinley is the highest peak in the U.S.
—it's 3½ miles high!

Sixty million years ago the mountain chain that
includes the Rockies in North America and the Andes in
South America rose up out of the sea. So don't be
surprised to find seashell fossils on top of these peaks.
(In the summer, that is!)

# Cross-Country Skiing

Some people feel that cross-country skiing is easier and more pleasant than downhill skiing. The terrain is far gentler, the stride is simple to learn, the equipment is lighter and more flexible, the vigorous exercise keeps you warm, and there are NO LIFT LINES! All you have to do is know where you're going, fit your toes into the bindings, and away you glide!

Keep a Nordic diary and a scrapbook of trail maps, touring center pamphlets or patches, and photos of your adventures on skis. Have a terrific touring time!

I've been cross-country skiing (circle)

once or twice     lots of times     for years

I started at the age of _____, and I learned/I'm learning by
(circle)

_____

_____

I can (circle)    walk    glide    diagonal stride    kick-turn

herringbone    side-step    skate    step-turn    snowplow stop

double-pole    telemark turn    parallel turn

I consider myself to be (circle)

a beginner    a novice    an intermediate

advanced    an expert    a racer

I usually ski with these people: _____

_____

What I like best about Nordic skiing is _____

_____

_____

_____.

What I *don't* like is _____

_____

_____

_____.

My favorite kind of trail is _____

_____

_____

_____.

On the average, we cover _____ miles/kilometers a day.
                                    (circle)

During this vacation/ski season, I'd like to learn how to _____
            (circle)

_____

_____

_____.

# Cross-Country Skiing Equipment

*Boots*

    Size: _____

    Brand: _____

    Style: _____

    Color: _____

    Comfortable? _____

*Bindings*

    Type: _____

    Brand: _____

*Skis*

    Type: _____

    Brand: _____

    Length: _____

Are your skis waxable or waxless? _____. If waxable, which

waxes did you use? _____

_____

_____

*Poles*

    Type: _____

    Length: _____

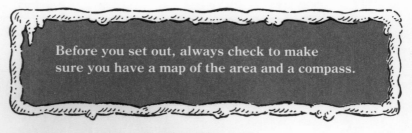

Before you set out, always check to make
sure you have a map of the area and a compass.

Use this page for a drawing or a photograph of you on your skis.

# Touring Centers

Date of tour #1: _____

Name of touring center or area: _____

_____

Location: _____

The elevation is _____.

Miles of tourable territory: _____

In the summer, this area is (circle)

      a farm     a golf course     campgrounds     horseback riding paths

      hiking or recreational trails     back-country or abandoned logging roads

      other: _____

The trails here are groomed/not groomed for cross-country skiing.
                    (circle)

The terrain is mostly _____

_____,

with a few areas of _____

_____.

The conditions were _____.

My favorite trails were _____

_____, because

_____

_____

During our tour, we saw _____

_____.

Overall, I like/don't like this area, because _____
      (circle)

_____

_____.

Date of tour #2: _____

Name of touring center or area: _____

_____

Location: _____

The elevation is _____.

Miles of tourable territory: _____

In the summer, this area is (circle)

      a farm     a golf course     campgrounds     horseback riding paths

      hiking or recreational trails     back-country or abandoned logging roads

      other: _____

The trails here are groomed/not groomed for cross-country skiing.
                      (circle)

The terrain is mostly _____

_____,

with a few areas of _____

_____.

The conditions were _____.

My favorite trails were _____

_____, because

_____

_____.

During our tour, we saw _____

_____.

Overall, I like/don't like this area, because _____
      (circle)

_____

_____

_____.

# My Adventures, Explorations, and Progress on Cross-Country Skis

First day out: _____

_____

_____

_____

Second day: _____

_____

_____

_____

Third day: _____

_____

_____

_____

Fourth day: _____

_____

_____

_____

Fifth day: _____

_____

_____

_____

Sixth day: _____

_____

_____

_____

In words and/or pictures, here were some of our most special, exciting, or challenging experiences.

Use these pages for trail maps, photographs (action shots are great), postcards, brochures, drawings, or other mementos of your cross-country outings. Or write down your thoughts about gliding through the winter woods.

"Touring appeals to the pioneer spirit, promotes self-reliance, and adds a real sense of adventure to your outings. It is a thrill to see wild animals or simply follow their tracks in fresh snow. And the winter scenery can be breathtaking."

Richard Lyttle, *The Complete Beginner's Guide to Skiing*

If you'd like to do some cross-country racing, check into the Bill Koch League, which sponsors competitions for kids aged 6–13. Bill Koch was the first American Olympic gold medalist in Nordic skiing. Contact your regional U.S. Ski Association's office for details.

# Ice Skating

I've been skating for _____ years/months/days. I started at the
(circle)

age of _____, and I learned/I'm learning by _____
(circle)

_____.

I can (circle)    skate forward      skate backward      glide on one foot

do forward crossovers      do backward crossovers      speed skate

snowplow stop      hockey stop      T-stop

I can also do (circle)    spirals      three-turns      spins      bunny hops

jumps      figure eights      other: _____

_____

_____

I consider myself to be (circle):      a beginner      a novice

an intermediate      advanced      an expert      an advanced expert

What I like best about skating is _____

_____

_____

_____

_____

What I *don't* like is _____

_____

The first ice skates were worn in Norway,
Sweden, and Finland over 2,000 years ago.
The blades were made of animal bones!

My favorite place to skate is _____

_____ ,

and I like skating to this kind of music: _____

I enjoy (circle)    playing ice hockey    speed skating    ice dancing

      skating arm-in-arm with a friend    playing ice tag

and sometimes, I like to _____

_____

_____ .

During this vacation, I'd like to learn how to _____

_____ .

*Someday,* I'd like to learn how to _____

_____ .

# Ice Skating

Here's a drawing or photograph of me on the ice:

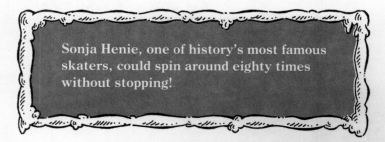

Sonja Henie, one of history's most famous skaters, could spin around eighty times without stopping!

# Other Frosty Sports

Write about them here!

We went sledding at _____

_____,

where the hills are _____

_____.

We used (circle)    runner sleds

flying saucers       inner tubes

a toboggan      a bobsled      a luge

a dogsled. Our sled was pulled by _____ dogs, who were named

_____

_____

_____.

We covered this much territory: _____

_____

We steered our sled(s) by _____

_____,

and we stopped by _____

_____.

The most exciting moment was

_____

_____

The most hilarious moment was _____

_____

We went snowshoeing at _____.

At first, the snowshoes felt _____, but eventually, I was

able to _____.

During our walk, we _____

_____

_____

_____

_____.

We went snowmobiling at _____.

Our average speed was _____ miles per hour, and we toured all over

_____.

Along the way we saw _____

_____.

The best part of our snowmobile trip was _____

_____

_____.

No sled? Some ski resorts hold "body sledding" contests each winter. Fearless folks wrap themselves in plastic and other slippery things and careen down the hill just like that! If body sledding seems a bit extreme, find a piece of corrugated cardboard and you'll be in business. Just rub the bottom of the cardboard with snow—or better yet, paste wax—and away you go!

We went ice fishing at _____

_____. We cut a

hole in the ice by _____

_____,

and while we waited for a bite, we ____

_____

_____.

(We kept warm by _____

_____.)

I caught _____ fish.
(number and type)

    We rode on a one-horse sleigh at _____.

Our horse was called _____.

The best part of the ride was _____

_____

_____

    We also went (circle)    on a "snow cat" tour    skibobbing

    swimming in a super-heated outdoor pool

    curling    snow golfing

    horseback riding

    ice sailing

    snowboarding

    other: _____

_____

_____
_____
_____

My favorite winter sports to watch are (circle)     downhill racing

grand slalom competitions     freestyle and ski-ballet competitions

cross-country racing     ski jumping     figure skating     ice dancing

speed skating     ice hockey     bobsledding     dogsled racing

other: _____

I especially like watching _____, because

_____

_____

_____ .

During this vacation we saw the following competition(s) or event(s): _____

_____

_____

The most interesting thing about it was _____

_____

_____

_____ .

Use these pages for drawings, photographs, or thrilling descriptions of your athletic adventures or the sports you watched!

# New Friends

To remember the kids you meet on vacation—on the trail, at the lodge, in lift lines, taking lessons, or toasting marshmallows at the bonfire—use these pages for addresses, autographs, and photos.

| Name | Address | Phone |
| --- | --- | --- |
|  |  |  |
|  |  |  |
|  |  |  |
|  |  |  |
|  |  |  |
|  |  |  |
|  |  |  |
|  |  |  |
|  |  |  |
|  |  |  |
|  |  |  |
|  |  |  |
|  |  |  |
|  |  |  |
|  |  |  |
|  |  |  |
|  |  |  |

ographs

# Photographs

s or drawings of new friends.

# An Informal Interview
## with a Skiing or Skating Instructor

If you take a skiing or skating lesson during your vacation, interview the instructor before or after your class. Even if you don't take a lesson, you can probably find a friendly instructor at the local ski or skating school counter.

Instructor's name: _____ Age: _____

Q: Where did you grow up?

A: _____

Q: Where do you live in the summer?

A: _____

Q: How long have you been a ski instructor/skating instructor?

A: _____

Q: When the season is over, do you have another profession?

A: _____

Q: How old were you when you learned how to ski/skate?

A: _____

Q: Who taught you?

A: _____

Q: What do you like the most about skiing/skating?

A: _____

_____

_____

Q: Where's your favorite place to ski/skate, and why?

A: _____

_____

_____

_____

Q: Have you ever entered any races or competitions? Which ones? Did you ever win any medals?

A: _____

_____

Q: What's your favorite fancy move?

A: _____

Q: What do you like best about teaching?

A: _____

Q: What don't you like about teaching?

A: _____

Q: What words of wisdom would you offer young skiers/skaters?

A: _____

_____

Instructor's autograph: _____

Use this space for a sketch or photo of the instructor.

# Winter Wildlife

Animals can be new acquaintances too. An early morning stroll through the woods (with an adult) might give you a chance to meet—or at least observe—the local fauna.

If you have a camera or binoculars, bring them along! You might also like to bring some nuts, raisins, lettuce, or bread crumbs to scatter. Be sure to walk softly and speak quietly as you proceed. Go slowly. Keep your eyes and ears open.

Below are some animals to look for. Naturally, the wildlife you see will depend on your geographical area and the type of environment you explore. A nature guidebook can tell you what species are local and help you identify their tracks in the snow. Check off the animals you saw and write about your woodland experiences on the following pages.

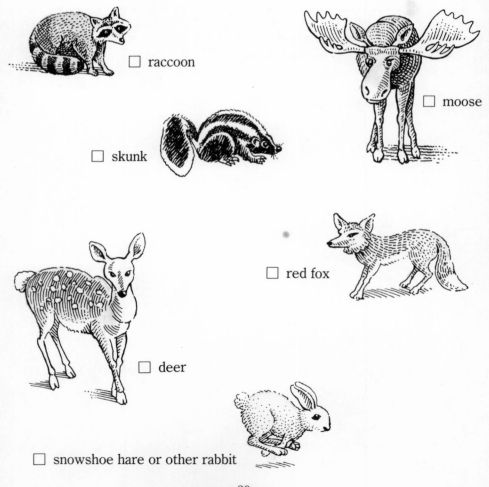

☐ raccoon

☐ moose

☐ skunk

☐ red fox

☐ deer

☐ snowshoe hare or other rabbit

 ☐ squirrel

☐ chipmunk

☐ weasel
(Its winter fur is white.)

 ☐ bighorn sheep

 ☐ elk

☐ beaver
(Look in half-frozen streams.)

 ☐ otter (Also found in streams.)

☐ non-migratory birds such as pine siskins, cardinals, blue jays, grouses, snowy owls, and hairy woodpeckers

# Winter Wildlife

Use these pages for a description of your walk in the woods or for drawings, photographs, stray bird feathers, or postcards of the animals you saw.

Some scientists did a study to determine which animal has the warmest winter coat. No, it's not your hairy Uncle Fred! Care to take another guess? It's the wolf!

Each fall, in anticipation of the snow, the ruffed grouse grows a mock snowshoe. Comblike fringes appear along the sides of the bird's feet. This makes walking in the snow easier. The grouse then molts the extra baggage in the spring. Pretty neat, huh?

When the Sun
Goes Down

You've just finished a full day of outdoor activity. Your cheeks are bright red. You feel incredibly healthy and fit. It's now time for what the French call "après-ski" (after skiing). Many people enjoy these relaxing or lively sundown hours as much as their day on the slopes.

You can explore the town or window-shop. See a movie. Visit a local art gallery or museum. Attend a bonfire, a hootenanny, an ice show, or a play. Take a moonlight sleigh ride. Or you can rest your weary muscles and spend a quiet evening at your home away from home. Have a sauna, a swim, or a nice hot bath. Play cards or games. Or curl up somewhere comfy and read a good book.

What do you like to do?

After a day of _____, I feel very _____

_____.

My favorite evening activity is _____,

because _____

_____.

I also like to _____

_____

_____

One evening, we _____

_____

_____

_____

_____.

# Exploring the Town

Check out your vacation village. In the evening, or on a "rest day" from the thrills and spills of winter sports, ramble into town and snoop around the streets. Collect information about the area. Get a brochure or two from the local tourist office or a hotel lobby, and ask questions—the natives are usually very friendly.

Name of the city, town, or village: _____

Year founded: _____

Does the town's name have a special meaning? (Is it named for an Indian tribe? An old silver mine?) _____

_____

Where is the village situated? (circle)

    at the foot of _____ Mountain

    in a valley    up on the mountainside

    other: _____

The first residents were _____, and for many years the town's principal industry was _____.

Other interesting facts about the town's history (important events, famous residents, memorable blizzards or avalanches): _____

_____

_____

_____

Population of the town today

    in tourist season: _____ off-season: _____

    (The difference is sometimes astonishing!)

What's the best way to get around town? (circle)

    on foot    on skis    by horse and sleigh    by shuttle bus

    other: _____

What does the town look like? Are there cobblestone streets? Victorian "gingerbread" houses? Alpine chalets perched on stilts against the mountainside? Describe the local architectural styles.

_____

_____

_____

_____

Are there any unusual landmarks in or near the town? An old mine? A weather station or observatory? _____

_____

_____

Do the people who live here speak another language? Which one(s)? _____ If so, what are some of the words you've learned or noticed on signs? What are their meanings? _____

_____

_____

Are there any local specialties—crafts, foods, or games? What are they?

_____

_____

_____

What's your favorite part of the town, and why? _____

_____

_____

Would you like to live here? _____ Why or why not? _____

_____

_____

_____

# Exploring the Town

Use these pages for postcards, photographs, and souvenirs of your visits to town.

# Shopping Around

At winter resorts, the stores can be a lot of fun—full of super sports equipment, elegant winter wear, unusual crafts, and mouth-watering treats. Record what you saw, what you bought, and what you would have *liked* to buy. Collect business cards from the niftiest emporiums.

Here are some of the strange and/or wonderful things I saw for sale:

_____

_____

_____

_____

_____

This is what I bought: _____

_____

_____

_____

_____

_____

Ski areas are famous for patches and pins. If you're starting a collection, store your prizes in the Memory Box.

This is what i would have *liked* to buy, but . . . oh, well.

_____

_____

My favorite shop was _____,

because _____

_____.

Business cards, labels, and other shopping paraphernalia:

# A Night at the Movies

These are the movies I saw on my vacation:

Title of movie: _____

Starring: _____

Subject or basic plot: _____

_____

My critique: _____

_____

_____

Title of movie: _____

Starring: _____

Subject or basic plot: _____

_____

My critique: _____

_____

_____

Title of movie: _____

Starring: _____

Subject or basic plot: _____

_____

My critique: _____

_____

Ticket stubs:

# Other Evening Excursions

What else did you do when you were out and about? Did you visit a museum or art gallery? Did you attend a square dance or a singalong? Immortalize your après-ski experiences here. Don't forget to paste in any memorabilia you've saved.

_____

_____

_____

_____

_____

_____

_____

_____

_____

_____

_____

_____

_____

_____

_____

_____

_____

_____

_____

_____

_____

_____

_____

_____

Use this space to continue your report or to glue in souvenirs from your evenings out.

Some resorts have a winter carnival every year, with sports exhibitions, cookouts, concerts, ice sculpture competitions, fireworks, and a torchlight parade. Were you lucky to catch a special holiday or festival during your vacation?

# Vacation Reading Diary

During my vacation, I read _____,

by _____.

It was about _____

_____

_____.

I enjoyed/didn't enjoy it, because _____
(circle)

_____

_____

_____.

I've also been reading: _____

_____

_____

_____

_____

_____

_____

_____

_____

Other interesting books or articles I read: _____

_____

_____

_____

_____

# Games

Here are some of the card games, board games, and video games I've been playing.

Game: _____ Players: _____

High scores, funny moments, or exciting plays: _____

_____

_____

Game: _____ Players: _____

High scores, funny moments, or exciting plays: _____

_____

_____

Game: _____ Players: _____

High scores, funny moments, or exciting plays: _____

_____

_____

Other games we've watched or played during our vacation: _____

_____

_____

_____

_____

_____

_____

_____

_____

_____

# The Official Tall Tale

You've probably heard the legend of the "Abominable Snowman"—that flat-faced, pointy-headed, hairy white critter that is said to live in the Himalayan Mountains. Tibetans affectionately refer to him as "Yeti" and believe he has magical powers.

Who knows what lurks in the shadows of the mountainside? Why don't you make up your own legend?

One morning, you get up early. You go outside. There are some strange footprints in the snow. The tracks lead to a cave in the deep forest. You peek into the entrance. Your mouth drops open in astonishment. What happens next?!

_____

_____

_____

_____

_____

_____

_____

_____

_____

_____

_____

_____

_____

_____

_____

_____

Here is a drawing of the creature I saw.

# The Time Machine

Imagine that it's 400 years into the future. You're visiting the same winter resort. What does it look like? What has changed? What are the snow sports of tomorrow? Do people still skate? Do they ski? How are they transported up the mountain?

The year is _____, and in the town of _____,

people now _____

_____

_____

_____

_____

_____

_____

_____

_____

_____

_____

_____

_____

_____

_____

_____

_____

_____

_____

_____.

Here's a drawing from the future.

# Special Times

# Nighttime on the Mountain

When you've got a perfectly clear night, bundle up, grab your companions, go outside, and star gaze. If you have a big tarpaulin or rain poncho, you can even settle into a snowbank for the full celestial view. You'll be treated to a skyful of stars, planets, and other astronomical sights. If you're lucky, you may see an aurora borealis (the "northern lights") or a meteor shower.

To distinguish between stars, planets, and satellites, keep these tips in mind: stars *do* twinkle, whereas the light from planets is much more constant. Satellites move steadily across the sky. And from December to April, the brightest constellation is Orion. See if you can find his sword and belt.

Use this space to record your observations.

Date: _____

Stargazers: _____

We saw: _____

_____

_____

_____

_____

_____

_____

_____

A wonderful book for aspiring astronomers is *The Night Sky Book* by Jamie Jobb.

# Alpine Dining

All that frosty air and exercise is bound to give you a moose-sized appetite! What have you done to stave off the hungry growls?

My favorite foods during this vacation were _____

_____

_____

_____.

The heartiest breakfast was at _____.

I had _____.

The best lunch was _____.

I thought the _____ was delicious!

The most scrumptious dinner was at _____.

I ate _____,

and for dessert I had _____.

In the early spring, when the sap of the maple tree begins to flow, the residents of Vermont, Quebec, and other maple-farming areas make a wonderful confection called "sugar in the snow." Hot maple syrup is dribbled onto fresh snow to make delicious lacy snowflakes. If you have a chance to attend a "sugaring off," try this wonderful treat! If not, make your own "snow cream." Set out a pan or bowl when it starts to snow. When you've collected an inch or two, add heavy cream, sugar, and vanilla extract. The result is mushy and delicious!

Here are some foods I tried for the first time: _____

_____

_____

_____

_____

The best was _____.

I also liked the _____,

but I thought the _____ tasted _____.

(By the way, please don't ever take me back to this restaurant: _____

_____)

> To perk up a mug of hot chocolate, add a cinnamon stick
> or a peppermint candy cane! Or try "hot vanilla" for a
> change. Warm up some milk with a little sugar or maple
> syrup, and add a piece of vanilla bean or a few drops of
> extract. Hot lemonade is also nice!

My favorite cold-weather drink is (circle)    hot chocolate    hot apple cider

      other: _____

and my favorite snacks to eat on the trail are _____

_____

_____

_____

_____

_____.

# Alpine Dining

Did you know that someone who collects matchbook covers is called a phillumenist? You can become a phillumenist, too, by gathering matchbooks from restaurants or hotels where you ate. Ask an adult to help you carefully remove and discard the matches, then glue the covers here! Or tape in photographs of snow picnics and other festive feasts!

# Special Memories

When you're back home again—shoveling the driveway or waiting for the spring, puzzling over a math problem or just drifting off to sleep—what will you remember about your vacation in this winter wonderland?

Use these pages to preserve your extra special mountain memories. Later you'll be able to pull out this book and . . . Presto! You'll be transported!

When I close my eyes I see these images of our vacation: _____

_____

_____

These sounds come to mind: _____

_____

These smells will remind me of vacation: _____

_____

Did you attend or participate in any special events—holiday celebrations, carnivals, parties, contests, festivals, pageants, or Olympic Games—while you were here?

Special events I'll always remember: _____

_____

_____

_____

_____

_____

This is *the* funniest thing that happened on vacation: _____

_____

_____

The most thrilling moment was _____

_____

_____.

The strangest/scariest/most embarrassing experience I had was _____
(circle)

_____

_____

_____

_____.

The latest we stayed up at night was _____ o'clock, and

the earliest we arose was _____ o'clock!

These are the words I'd use to describe this vacation (circle)

exciting        exhausting        relaxing

energetic        too long        too short

other: _____

# Special Memories

Did you have any special times with your traveling companions—good conversations, shared adventures? Record them here in words and/or pictures.

_____

_____

_____

_____

_____

_____

_____

_____

_____

_____

_____

_____

_____

_____

_____

_____

_____

The world's largest amateur ski race is the Firefighter's Race at Hunter Mountain, New York. Each team is made up of five firefighters who take to the downhill course with a fifty-foot fire hose! Can you imagine this scene?

# Other Special Memories

Use these pages for a scene from your winter wonderland—a drawing, photograph, or postcard of majestic peaks, snow-laden evergreens, fresh snowbanks, happy skiers, graceful skaters, or other seasonal sights.

Saying Good-bye

# A Final Vacation Questionnaire

Here's something to do on the way home.

What was absolutely the best part of this vacation?

_____

_____

_____


What was the worst part, if any? (circle)

      freezing                falling           sharing the bathroom

      waiting on lift or food lines        someone's snoring

      putting on all my sports clothing and equipment

      other: _____

      _____


What will you miss about your winter wonderland? (circle)

      the snow-covered mountains

      the clean, crisp air

      skiing, skating, or sledding every day

      the huge and delicious meals

      other: _____

      _____

      _____

# A Final Vacation Questionnaire

Was there anything you spotted in your snowy travels that you would have loved to take home with you but couldn't because (circle)

> your dad is allergic to them
>
> your suitcase would never have closed
>
> it was too expensive
>
> your backyard is too small for a ski jump
>
> other: _____

So, what was it??? And why did you want to take it home?

_____

_____

_____

_____

_____

On the average, how has the weather been during your vacation? (circle)

mostly sunny

cold enough to freeze nose hair

gray, with occasional snowfalls

blizzardy

frosty but pleasant

rainy and miserable

so foggy and misty the world was invisible

warm enough for a bathing suit

other: _____

Did you learn to do something new? What? _____

_____

_____

_____

Did you develop a new interest that you'd like to continue to pursue when you

get home?

What is it? _____

_____

If you ever return to this resort, what would you like to do that you didn't

have time for on this trip? _____

_____

_____

Did you remember to thank your traveling companions and/or hosts for a
wonderful time? (A note or a drawing would be a delightful thank-you!)

☐ Yes, I'm very polite.

☐ Oops, I forgot, but I'll do it right now.

# The Grand Vacation Awards

Here are the winners!

The Abominable Snowman Award, for the most falls taken in one vacation:

_____

The Hungry Lumberjack Award, for eating the most food at every meal:

_____

The Toasted Toes Award, for the most time spent by the fireplace in the
lodge: _____

The Snoozing Beauty Award, for sleeping the latest in the morning: _____

_____

The Jack Frostbite Award, for the numbest ears and fingers this side of the
Arctic Circle: _____

_____

The Silver Skates Award, for the smoothest maneuvers on ice: _____

_____

The Molasses in January Award, for the restaurant with the slowest service: _____

The Slippery Skier Award, for having fallen off the chairlift, tangled up the ropetow, or tripped over the T-bar before starting up the mountain: _____

_____

The Hotshot Hot Dog Award for the most impressive action on skis: _____

_____

And finally, The _____ Award, for

_____,

goes to _____.

A round of applause, please! Let's give them all a big hand!

# Three Cheers!

Write three cheers about your winter vacation.

#1   S is for _____!

N is for _____!

O is for _____!

W is for _____!

#2   _____

_____

_____

#3   _____

_____

_____

# The "After" Photo

Okay! Here's the space for a photograph of the new you—rested, refreshed, and looking great!

# Extra Pages

Use the following pages for drawings, stories, photographs, poems, game scores, postcards, ticket stubs, brochures, pamphlets, ski passes, mementos, and anything else you created or collected during your trip!

# Extra Pages

Sketch it! Snap it! Tape it! Put it here!

# More Stuff!